JAKE MADDOX
GRAPHIC NOVELS

STONE ARCH BOOKS
a capstone imprint

JAKE MADDOX
GRAPHIC NOVELS

Published by Stone Arch Books,
an imprint of Capstone.
1710 Roe Crest Drive
North Mankato, Minnesota 56003
www.capstonepub.com

Library of Congress Cataloging-in-Publication Data
Names: Hoena, B. A., author. | Papalia, Roberta, artist. | Reed, Jaymes, letterer. | Muñiz, Berenice, cover artist.
Title: Running wild / text by Blake Hoena ; art by Roberta Papalia ; lettering by Jaymes Reed ; cover art by Berenice Muñiz.
Description: North Mankato, Minnesota : Stone Arch Books, [2021] | Series: Jake Maddox graphic novels | Audience: Ages 8–11. | Audience: Grades 4–6. | Includes discussion questions, notes about obstacle courses, and glossary.
Identifiers: LCCN 2020025518 (print) | LCCN 2020025519 (ebook) | ISBN 9781515882329 (library binding) | ISBN 9781515883418 (paperback) | ISBN 9781515892243 (eBook PDF)
Subjects: LCSH: Graphic novels. | CYAC: Graphic novels. | Farm life—Fiction. | Running—Fiction. | Obstacle racing—Fiction.
Classification: LCC PZ7.7.H64 Run 2021 (print) | LCC PZ7.7.H64 (ebook) | DDC 741.5/973—dc23
LC record available at https://lccn.loc.gov/2020025518
LC ebook record available at https://lccn.loc.gov/2020025519

Summary: Toby Brandt is nervous about his basketball injury. But he's about to gain some new confidence and an appreciation for the great outdoors. When his cousin Chloe and her friends convince him to join in their nature runs, he learns to enjoy running in the woods and through their homemade obstacle course. Will Toby overcome his fears in time for the local Wild Run and win the biggest, sloppiest mud race around?

Editor: Aaron Sautter
Designer: Brann Garvey
Production Specialist: Tori Abraham

Printed and bound in the USA. PO 3837

RUNNING WILD

Text by Blake Hoena

Art by Roberta Papalia

Color by Francesca Ingrassia
(Grafimated Cartoon)

STARTING LINEUP
TOBY
CHLOE

LIZZY
JACKSON
GRANDPA JON

Number 34, Toby Brandt,
is wide open . . .
. . . he gets the ball . . .
. . . he jukes one
defender . . .

. . . and drives into the lane . . .
. . . he goes up . . .
. . . he shoots . . .
. . . and it's . . .
Hey, we're here!

Come on, Toby. Wake up!
Huh? Wh-wha . . . where are we?
We're at the farm!
What am I going to do out here in the middle of nowhere?
It'll be a big change from the city.
Yeah, right. No fun and lots of chores.
But Chloe will be excited to see you.

Hey, coz!
Whoa! WHOA! Careful, Chloe.
Remember, I hurt my ankle.
Yeah, like months ago. But I thought the doc said you didn't need that anymore.
I've been wearing my walking boot as a precaution. You know, just to be safe.

Okay, sorry, coz . . .
You remember Lizzy and Jackson, don't you?
Hey, Tobes!
Been a while.
Yeah, it's been ages since I've been out here on Grandpa Jon's farm.
So after that long ride, you wanna stretch your legs a bit and join us?
What do you have planned?

We're going for a trail run.
It's pretty hardcore if you're up for it.
Yeah, let's see what Mr. Basketball Star can do.
Thanks, but, better not. You know, not with my ankle and all.
Well if you aren't going with them, you can bring your bags inside.

But my ankle . . .
Then use your hands. That's what the *handles* are for.
Once you're settled in, I have some chores that need doin' before supper.
But . . .
That is, unless you plan to meet up with Chloe and her friends.
They'll probably be over by the river.

A little later . . .
I can't believe my folks sent me here for the summer.
I should be at home resting my leg. *And* I shouldn't be doing chores out here on the farm . . .
Is that them?
Come on! Last one across has dish duty!

Wow! They're running across the river.
SPLASH!
SLOSH! SLOSH!
SLOSH! SLOSH!
First!
Second!
Aw, man! I'm on dish duty, *again*?
huff . . .
Hey, Tobes, . . .
huff, huff . . . you're missing out on the fun.

That looks pretty wild.
Feel free to join us.
I dunno . . . maybe later. You know, if my ankle feels okay.
Okay, well, we need to get in some practice miles. The Wild Run is coming up next weekend.
The Wild Run? What's that?
Oh, it's a big obstacle race that's held every year.
People come from all over to compete. It's a blast.
Well, gotta run! See you back at the farm!

Later that evening . . .
So what happened to your ankle?
Yeah, Chloe told us you busted it up pretty bad.
He did it while scoring the winning basket in some game.
Some game?!
It was the conference championship!
SWISH!
Just after going up for the game-winning shot . . .

. . . I came down, hard, on someone's foot.
POP!
While my teammates celebrated, I was in agony. My ankle was fractured.
I had to be carried off the court.
Whoah, that blows.

But it's better now, right?
Yeah, I guess. The doctor gave me the greenlight to do whatever I want. But . . .
Hey, no "buts" around here.
The Doc gave you a clean bill of health. And I've got some hay that needs to be baled tomorrow.
Yup, no escaping chores around here.
Speaking of . . . I'm on dish duty.
House Rule #1. Grandpa Jon feeds us, and we take care of the dishes.

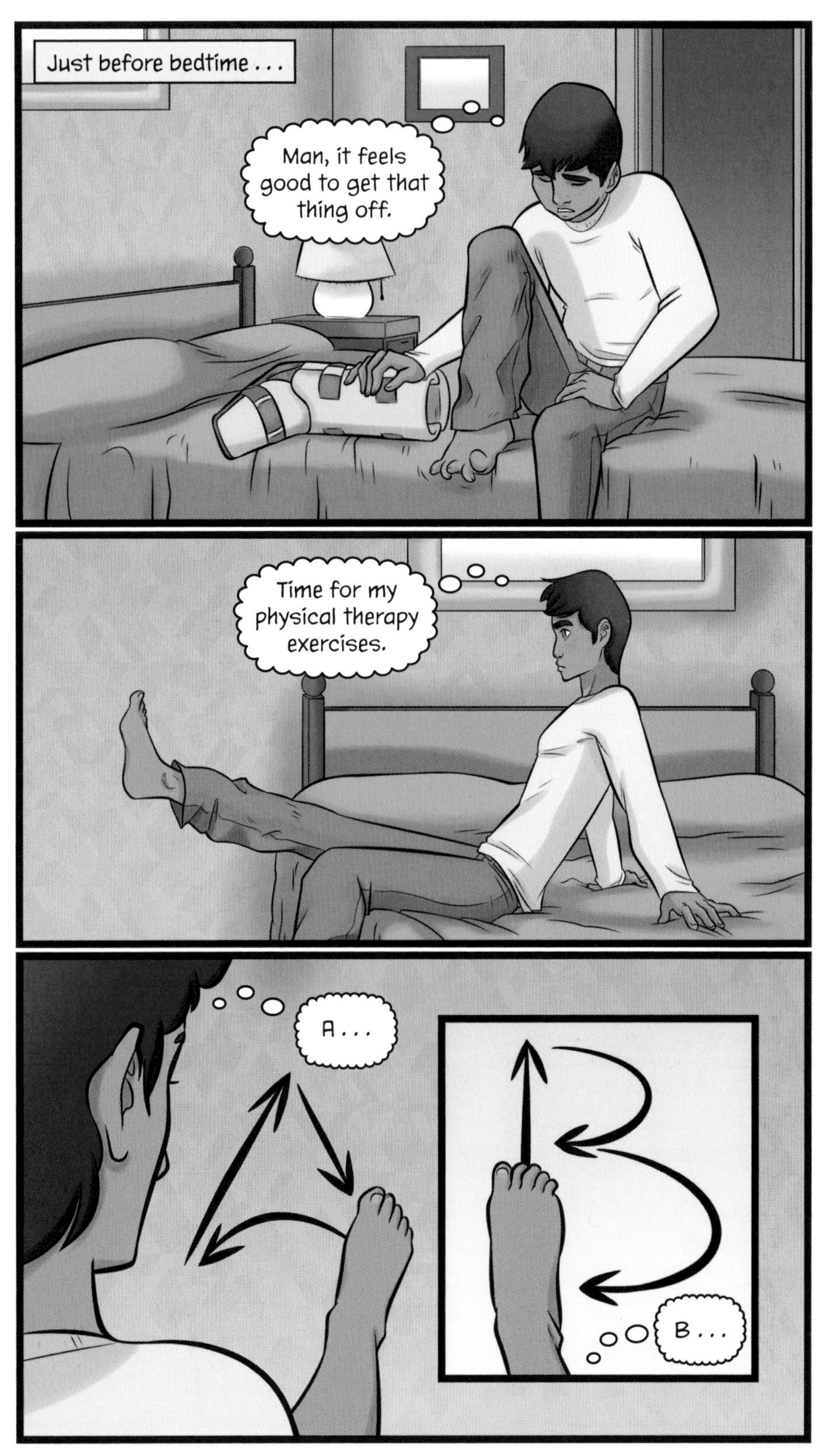
Just before bedtime . . .
Man, it feels good to get that thing off.
Time for my physical therapy exercises.
A . . .
B . . .

The next day . . .
How are you two doin' back there?
Just . . . *grunt* . . . fine!
You need help with that?
They're just heavier than . . . *grunt* . . . I remember.

And this boot isn't helping any.
CLUNK!
Straw keeps getting in it, and it itches like crazy.
skritch skritch
Hay.
Hey, what?
No, city boy, these are bales of *hay*. Not straw.

Aren't they. . . *grunt* . . . the same thing?
Hay is green and used to feed the animals. Straw is all dried up and used for bedding.
I think you've been living out here with Grandpa Jon too long.
You used to love coming out to the farm.
Before the big city . . . *grunt* . . . and basketball.
This thing keeps bugging me.

Just take it off then. You don't need it.
But, my ankle . . . I don't want to hurt it.
Fine then. You could do something less itchy like, maybe . . .
. . . shoveling out the cow manure in the barn.
Besides, how will you know if your ankle is healed if you keep babying it?
Okay! Okay!

Good job, you two! We're done with this field.
Bet you haven't worked that hard in ages.
Nah, if I was back home, I'd just be working out at the rec center or shooting hoops.
If my ankle was up for it, that is.
Looks like your friends think they can get you out of your chores.

Hey, you two done for the day?
We were hoping to go for another run.
Can I go? This field's cleared.
Yeah, sure. Get out of here.
And what about you? You going, too?
I . . . um . . .

If not, you can help me unload this back at the barn.
Well . . .
See ya later Grandpa!
Come on. We need to head back and gear up.
Hey, Toby, why aren't you wearing your walking boot?
You must have left it on the wagon.

Think I should go get it?
If you do, Grandpa Jon's just going to put you to work.
Here, you'll need this.
I don't know if I should . . .
Grandpa Jon's on his way back.
Let's go! Or else it's chores for all of us.

I'm coming,
I'm coming.
Wait up!
I'll take
the lead.
Don't think
you'll get out
of dish duty
that easily!

We're heading in there?
Wait until you see the obstacles we've set up.
I don't know about this . . .

Keep up if you can.
He always burns himself out early.
Careful of the tree up ahead.
The what?!

WHOOSH!
WHOOSH!
SSShhKKKSShh!
Not so fast! I don't want to hurt my ankle.

HUFF! HUFF!
HUFF! HUFF!
HUFF! HUFF!
Are you serious?
We're running up that?

Come on, you can do it!
Just a little farther!
umpf!
Grab my hand.
Hey, man, you made it!
Yeah, I did, didn't I?
But the fun is just beginning.

Last one across does dishes!
Hey, no fair!
SPLASH!
SLOSH! SLOSH!
SLOSH! SLOSH!

First!
Second!
Third!
Gah! Dishes, *again*!

How you holding up?
I'm okay. I just haven't run like that since . . .
. . . well, since I hurt my ankle.
And the fun's not over.
My turn to lead!
What's next?
Grandpa Jon let us set up an obstacle course in an empty field.

Come on! You'll have a blast.
I . . . can't wait!

How do we get through that?
We don't go *through* it!
We go *under!*
What's next?
Follow me!

Don't fall . . .
don't fall . . .
don't fall!
urgh . . .
grunt

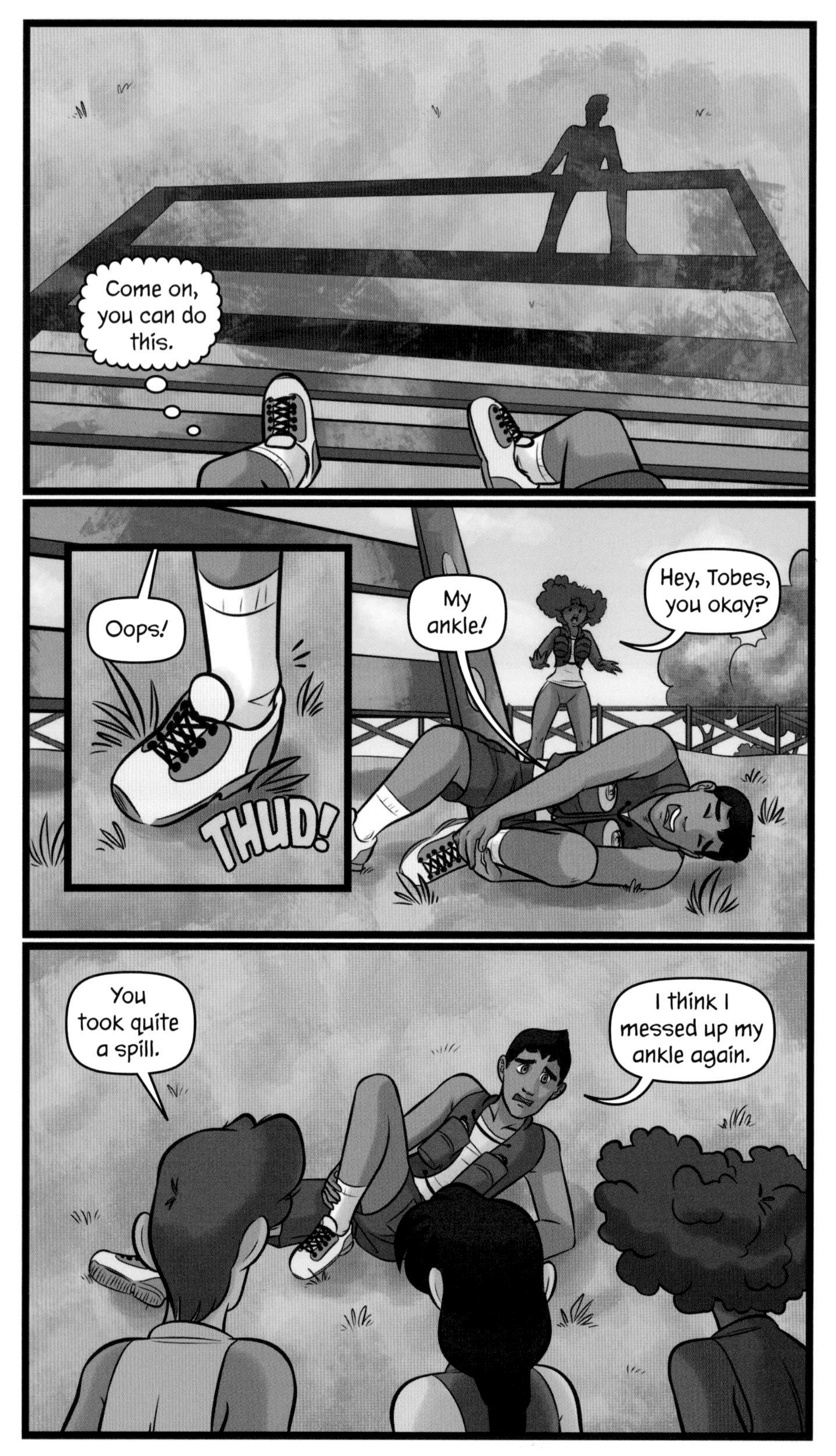
Come on, you can do this.
Oops!
THUD!
My ankle!
Hey, Tobes, you okay?
You took quite a spill.
I think I messed up my ankle again.

But that isn't your injured ankle.
Oh. Yeah.
How's it feel?
Let me try to walk it off and see.
Think he's going to be okay?
I dunno.

Let's go!
Sports drinks?
Yeah.
Me, too.

So what'd you think?
That was fun. But why are you doing this?
We're getting ready for the Wild Run. Didn't Chloe mention it?
Yeah! It's a BLAST! We do it every summer.
We participate as a team. It's a lot of fun. You want to run with us?
I dunno . . . maybe.

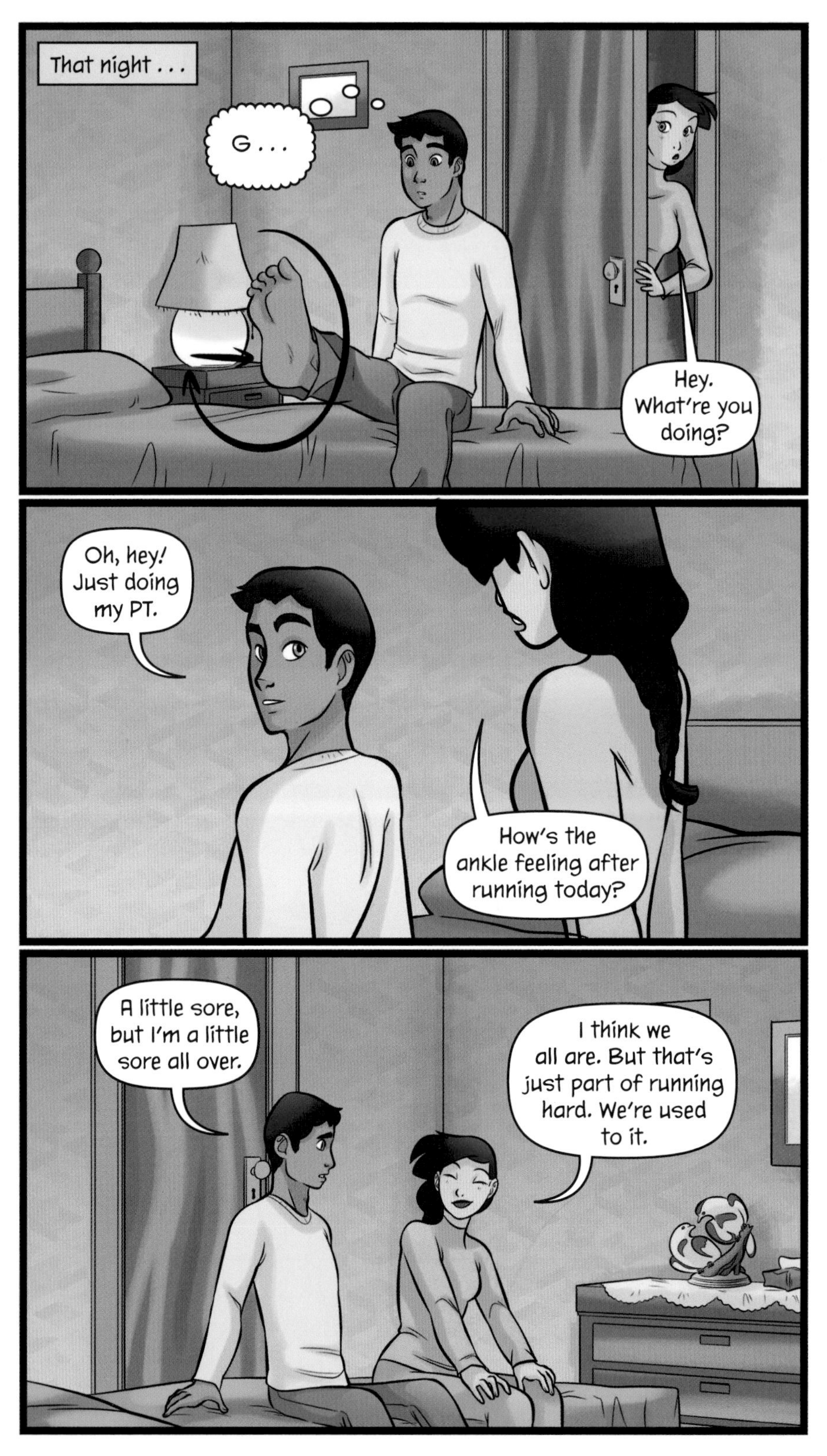
That night . . .
G . . .
Hey. What're you doing?
Oh, hey! Just doing my PT.
How's the ankle feeling after running today?
A little sore, but I'm a little sore all over.
I think we all are. But that's just part of running hard. We're used to it.

Listen, I didn't want to pressure you into doing the Wild Run. I just thought it'd be fun. But if you're worried about getting hurt . . .
It's not that. I just don't want to let you down. Like I let my team down.
What do you mean?
You know, we were down a player because I couldn't play. Then we lost the next game, the regional championship.
If I get hurt, I'll let you guys down too.

Listen, you didn't let your team down. You got hurt. That wasn't your fault.
I know, but . . .
Don't worry about it. We're just racing for fun. . . . although it'd be nice to beat the kids from Rusk.
Besides, you're pretty fast when you aren't worrying about your ankle. So just think about it.
I did have a blast today.

The next day . . .
I'm surprised you remember how to do that.
SQUIRT!
Just like riding a bike.
Are you kids finished with the milking?
Almost. We just need to clean up.
You guys up for a run today?
Is that okay Grandpa?
Yeah, yeah, go on. I'll finish up here.
Thanks, Grandpa!

Over the next week . . .
Okay, so this is straw, not hay?
You got it! We're gonna make a real farm boy out of you yet.
First!
Second!
Third!
Oh, man . . . Dishes!

I dunno about this.
Don't worry! It's not a race car. We're barely moving.
CHUG! CHUG! CHUG!
Look at you go!

Two days before the Wild Run . . .
So are we running again tomorrow?
Nah. We'd better rest up for the big race.
Yeah, we've been out almost every day since you got here, Tobes.
We need to give our legs a break before race day.
So how's the ankle been holding up?
My ankle? . . . Oh, yeah. I really haven't thought about it.

Am I feeding all of you kids tonight?
My uncle's taking me out for pizza.
Thanks, but I have dinner plans with my folks.
Then who's on dish duty?
That'd be me!

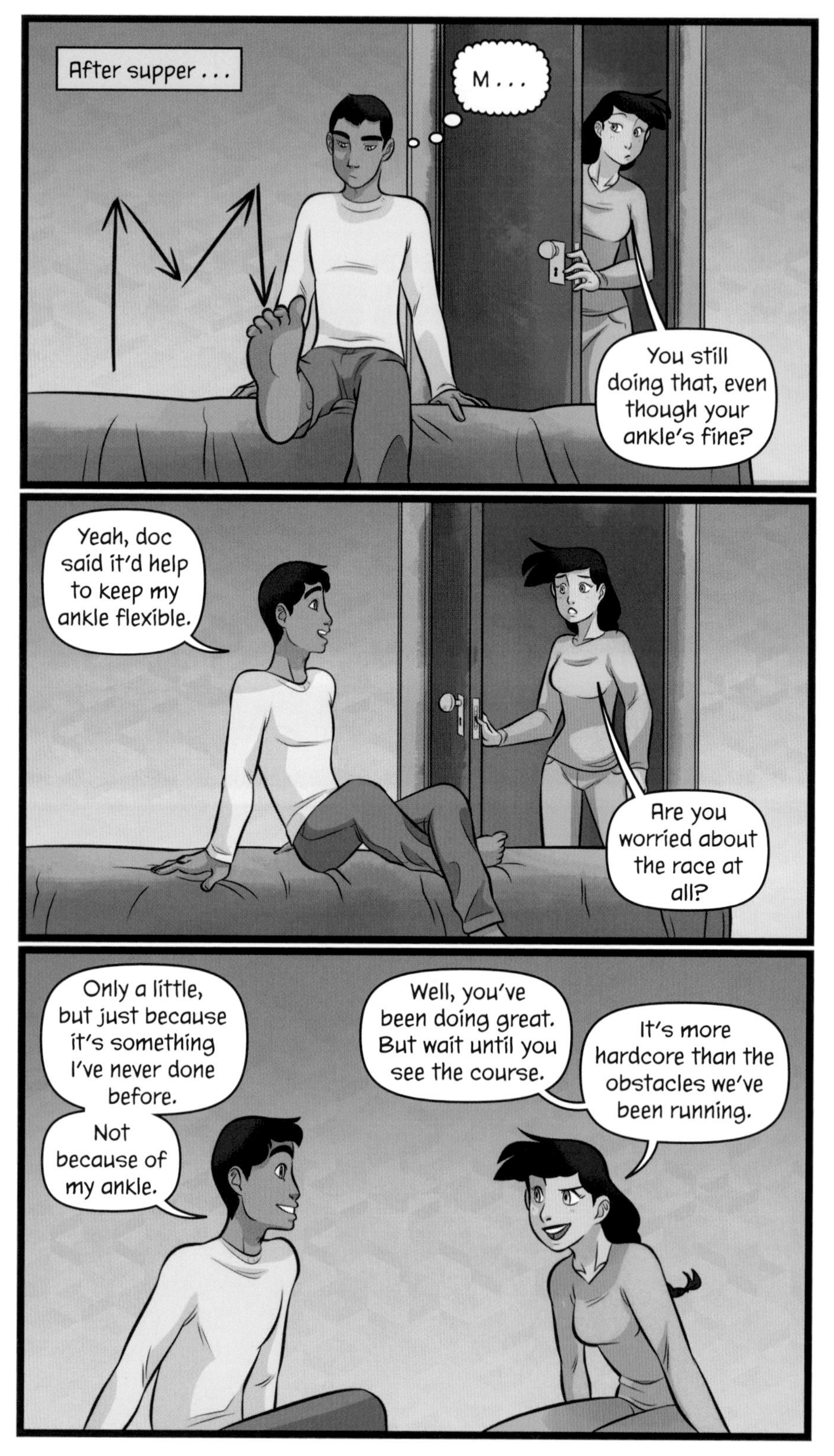
After supper . . .
M . . .
You still doing that, even though your ankle's fine?
Yeah, doc said it'd help to keep my ankle flexible.
Are you worried about the race at all?
Only a little, but just because it's something I've never done before.
Not because of my ankle.
Well, you've been doing great. But wait until you see the course.
It's more hardcore than the obstacles we've been running.

On race day . . .
WILD RUN
The race is five miles long with 20 obstacles.
1. Log Jump and Duck
2. Mud Pit
3. Slip and Slide
4. Monkey Crossing
5. Just a Puddle!
6. Fenced In
7. Roll With It
8. Moat Crossing
9. Getting Tired?
10. Muddier Pit
11. Mystery Obstacle
12. Mud Dip
13. Top That!
14. Getting Fishy?
15. Pinball
16. Get up!
17. Belly Crawl
18. Frog Hollow
19. Straw Mountain
20. Slime Tunnels
S
F

Those are the kids from Rusk.
They beat us last year.
Attention . . . runners 16 and under, your start time is in 15 minutes.
We'd better get ready.

Runners get ready!
Prepare to get muddy.
Yeah, they like to dirty us up in these races.
Get set!
HOOOOOON!

And the 16 and under runners are off!
WHOOSH!
That's one obstacle down, 19 to go!
SSShhkkkSShh!

What's next?
A mud pit!
Whoa! You guys didn't have this on your course!
SPLAT!
SPLAT!
The fun is just beginning!
I wonder what's coming next?

OOF!
I can barely hold on with all the mud on my hands.
SPLAT!
Whoa!
SHLLPP!

You okay? How's your ankle?
My wha— Hey, those are some of the Rusk kids.
Come on! We have to catch up.
THUMP!

Don't fall.
Don't fall.
I think I have mud in my ears.
I got some up my nose!
WEEE!!!
WEEE!!!
SHLORP!

Grab my hand!
Thanks!
THUD!
Now I got mud in my nose too!

Have you seen Jackson and Lizzy?
They're a ways back.
There's one of the kids from Rusk.
Let's pass him!

There's only one obstacle left!
What's that?
The Slime Tunnels!
WEEEE!!!!
SLOSH!
Hooo, boy! That was a blast!

You did it!
FINISH
Alright!
Woo-hoo!
SLAP!
That was awesome!
SLAP!

A little while later . . .
So the ankle didn't bother you?
Once we got going, I didn't even think about it.
Can't wait to tell my teammates about all of this.
Bet they'll be happy to hear you're ready for the upcoming season.
But now, after that race all I can think about is food.
Me, too!
Glad you kids had fun. But before anyone eats, it's shower time!
FFWIIISH!
The end.

1. Early in the story, Toby is nervous about doing anything that might reinjure his ankle. Compare his expressions in these two panels. How can you tell that Toby is no longer nervous about his ankle?

2. Graphic novel artists use different styles of art to tell a story. What clues in this panel tell you that it might be a dream?

3. Sometimes a character acts differently from what they say. Grandpa Jon seems hard on Toby and always tells him there are chores to be done. But does he really act tough on Toby and his friends?

4. Look at the map of the obstacles from the Wild Run. Which ones seem the most fun to you? Which seem the most difficult? How does the artwork help you decide?

Obstacle courses have their roots in the military. As far back as the Roman Empire, part of a soldier's training involved jumping over fences and climbing ropes. Even today, soldiers run obstacle courses to help them stay fit.

Obstacle courses test a person's strength, endurance, and mental toughness. They can involve running, jumping, climbing, crawling, swimming, and more. Some obstacles may need teamwork to conquer or involve problem solving. Courses are designed to mimic the challenges a soldier might face on a mission.

In 1900, an obstacle race was part of the Summer Olympics. Competitors swam a 200-meter course with three obstacles. They included climbing a pole, climbing over boats, and swimming under other boats. Fred Lane of Australia completed the course in 2 minutes, 38 seconds to win the gold medal.

By the 1950s, people began to realize the benefits of physical fitness as part of their daily lives. Universities in the United States began using military-style obstacle courses in their physical fitness programs. The Boy Scouts also set up obstacle courses at summer camps for their members.

Obstacle course racing took off as a competitive sport in the 1980s. It likely started with the 1987 Tough Guy race held in the United Kingdom. It was organized by ex-British soldier Billy Wilson. He set up a race to test competitors' physical and mental limits. The course included running through freezing cold water and smoke bombs exploding overhead. Today, the Tough Guy is considered one of the toughest obstacle courses in the world. About one third of all racers fail to finish.

Since the first Tough Guy race, many other obstacle racing events have popped up. One of the most popular is the Tough Mudder. This competition claims to be the "biggest, baddest, most epic obstacle course event." A full race is 10 miles (16 kilometers) long and includes more than 20 obstacles. The obstacles range from crossing a pond using a tightrope to the Hero Carry, in which two racers take turns carrying each other.

The Spartan Races are also popular. Their Beast races are 12 to 14 miles (19 to 22.5 km) long and include more than 30 obstacles. Competitors have to cross a mud-filled pit while hanging from various objects like rings, bars, and even balls attached to ropes. These objects are usually slippery and covered in mud from other competitors.

The Tough Mudder and Spartan Race are just two of the many obstacle course events being held around the world. There are races for almost everyone. Some are only a couple of miles long with a dozen obstacles. Grueling adventure races can be 100 miles (161 km) long and can include climbs over a 100-foot (30.5-meter) cliff or canoeing through river rapids. While these races are physically and mentally demanding, people enjoy the challenge of the obstacles. They take a lot of pride in overcoming these obstacles.

GLOSSARY

bale (BAYL)—a large bundle of hay or straw tied tightly together

chore (CHOHR)—a job that has to be done regularly; washing dishes and taking out the garbage are chores

conference (KAHN-fuhr-uhns)—a group of sports teams, often from nearby towns and schools

coz (CUZ)—short for cousin

defender (di-FEND-uhr)—a player on a team who tries to stop opposing players from scoring

fracture (FRAK-chur)—a broken or cracked bone

juke (JOOK)—to use a fake move to deceive a defending player

lane (LAYN)—the painted area on a basketball court under the hoop

obstacle course (OB-stuh-kuhl KORSS)—a type of race course with a series of barriers or objects that runners must jump over, climb, or crawl through

PT (PEE TEE)—short for physical therapy; any activity done to help someone recover from an injury

regional (REE-juh-nuhl)—a group of sports teams from a large area of a state

walking boot (WAW-king BOOT)—a stiff boot that helps support an injured foot or leg

Blake Hoena spent a chunk of his youth running around on a farm in central Wisconsin. It's where he developed his love of animals and the outdoors. He now lives in the big city of St. Paul, Minnesota, with his wife and a bunch of cats and dogs. When he's not writing, he spends his time outside, running or mountain biking on nearby trails.

Roberta Papalia was born in Catania, Italy, in 1995. After high school, she studied dentistry, but decided to pursue a career in art instead. Roberta studied comic art and animation at Grafimated Cartoon, part of the Palermo School of Comics in Palermo, Italy, and graduated in 2019. Roberta loves to draw and read comics of all types, playing role-playing games, and enjoys several other art forms. Today she lives near Catania with her pet python and two cats.

Berenice Muñiz is a graphic designer and illustrator from Monterrey, Mexico. She has done work for publicity agencies, art exhibitions, and even created her own webcomic. These days, Berenice is devoted to illustrating comics as part of the Graphikslava crew.

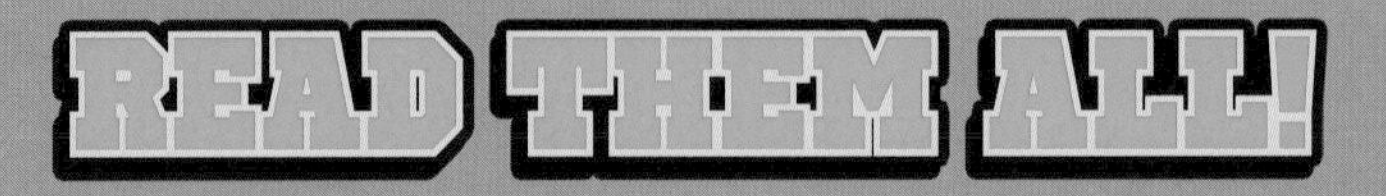

JAKE MADDOX
GRAPHIC NOVELS
COMEBACK CATCHER

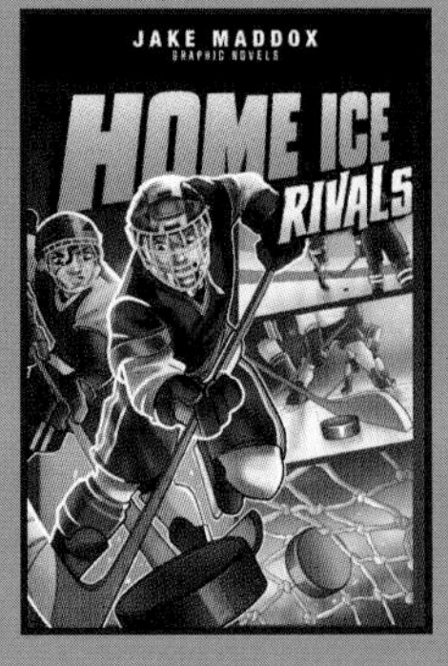

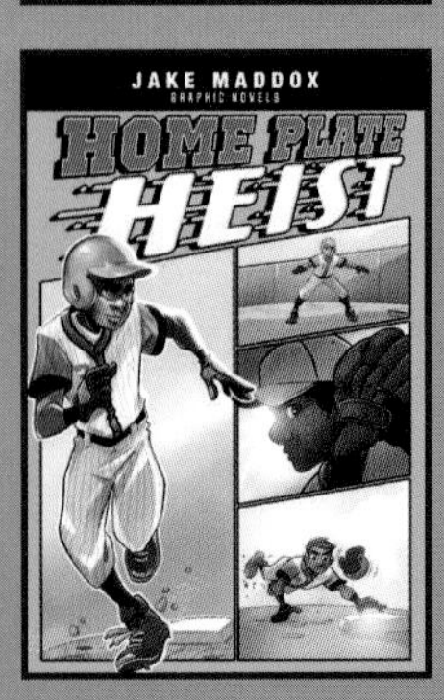

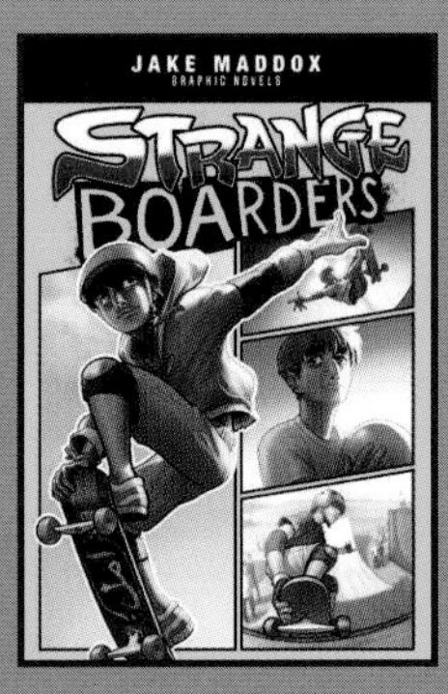